Get up, To...!

Written by John Townsend
Illustrated by Anna Shuttlewood

Collins

The sun is up.

Get up, Tom!

Cat sits on top.

Cat is up. Get up, Tom!

Dog tugs at a sock.

Dog is up. Get up, Tom!

Tom tips up a cup.

Tom is sad.

Pick it up, Tom.

Get a rag, Tom.

The sun is up, Cat is up
and Dog is up.

Up ... up ... up ... Tom is up!

A story map

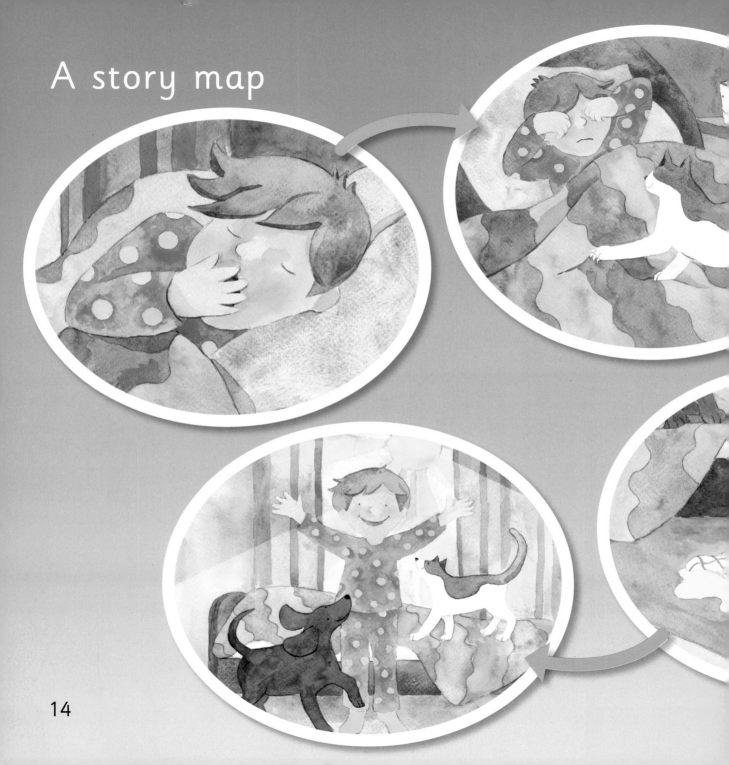

Ideas for reading

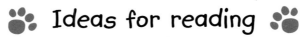

Written by Clare Dowdall, PhD
Lecturer and Primary Literacy Consultant

Learning objectives: read simple words by sounding out and blending the phonemes all through the word from left to right; read some high frequency words; read a range of familiar and common words and simple sentences independently; extend their vocabulary, exploring the meanings and sounds of new words; retell narratives in the correct sequence, drawing on the language patterns of stories; use talk to organise, sequence and clarify thinking, ideas, feelings and events; use phonic knowledge to write simple regular words

Curriculum links: Understanding the World: The world

Focus phonemes: g, o, c, n, ck, e, u, r

Fast words: the, is

Word count: 64

Getting started

- Read the title. Discuss the use of the comma and exclamation mark and model how to read the title with expression.

- Look at the front cover together. Ask children to describe what happens when they wake up in the morning and to describe what is happening to Tom.

- Ask children to predict what might happen in this story. Develop their vocabulary and support their speech, by using questions.

- Read the blurb together. Help children to recognise the fast words *the* and *is*. Model how to sound out the word *s-u-n*, and to blend the phonemes to read the word.

Reading and responding

- Read pp2–5 together. Look at the word *cat*. Revise the phoneme *c* by asking children to make its action, sound and to draw the grapheme in the air.

- Challenge the children to add sound buttons to the words *c-a-t* and *t-o-p* and to practise blending the sounds to read the words fluently.

- Ask the children to read to p13 aloud. Encourage them to blend phonemes to read new words fluently, and to use expression in their voice.

- Support the children as they read, moving around the group and intervening where necessary to praise, encourage and help.